Journeys of Courage
ON THE UNDERGROUND RAILROAD

Written by Darwin McBeth Walton
With Glennette Tilley Turner

STECK-VAUGHN
A Harcourt Company

www.steck-vaughn.com

Contents

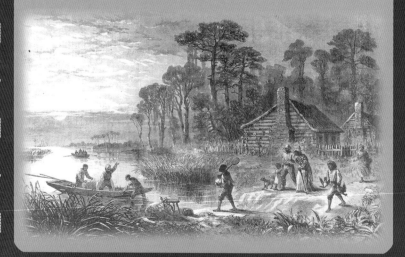

Chapter 1

Why the Underground Railroad Began

In 1619 nineteen Africans arrived in Jamestown, Virginia, on a ship. These Africans came to North America as **indentured** servants. Indentured servants were people who agreed to work without pay for seven years rather than go to jail for debts they couldn't pay. The captain of the ship had paid the Africans' debts and had let them travel on his ship. Once the ship reached Jamestown, the captain traded the Africans to planters for food and supplies.

As time passed, planters in all thirteen British colonies used indentured servants to work on their farms and **plantations.** Many of these servants were white. They worked for seven years and then were free to find jobs that paid **wages.** No laws protected indentured servants. For many Africans, seven years often turned into a lifetime of work without pay. That was how **slavery** started in North America.

3

Slavery had been practiced for thousands of years in all parts of the world, including Africa. People of one African **tribe** often captured people of an enemy tribe and made those people their slaves. But African slavery was a different kind of **bondage.** Because the slaves and the captors were of the same race, African slaves were accepted into the tribe and allowed to live like anybody else. They couldn't go back home, but they could marry and raise a family. They lived by using their talents and skills.

When slave trading became **profitable,** some African tribes kidnapped enemy tribes and sold them to European slave traders. The kidnappers stole clothing, jewelry, and anything else that would let others know the name and tribe of the captured people.

Africans were often sold at slave auctions.

4

The slave traders bound the captured people in iron chains, loaded them on ships, and then sold them as slaves. Many tried to escape. Some jumped overboard and drowned rather than be sold into slavery.

Some stories lead people to believe that Africans were happy being slaves. Why, then, did so many try to run away? The answer lies in what slavery was like.

Africans in America were not treated as **intelligent** people with hopes, feelings, and human needs. They had no control over the way they lived. They were not paid for their work. If they had special talents or skills, their owners hired them out and took the money they earned.

Many slaves and their children had a very hard life. They had to work very hard so that their owners could grow rich and have a good life. The slaves were given barely enough food to keep them alive and able to work. If a slave had a kind owner, the slave might have two changes of clothes for winter and two for summer. Most clothing was made of rough cloth, so it was not very comfortable. Slaves had to wear the clothes until they were rags.

Many slaves lived in shacks or one-room cabins with dirt floors. Many slaves had no beds. They slept on corn shucks or pine needles piled on the floor. Some slaves were given one thin blanket in winter. Other slaves had no blanket.

Some slaves had a better life than others. Through the years, some used their skills to improve the way they lived. They made furniture and clothes and grew their own vegetables. But they still couldn't plan for the future. They couldn't go anywhere without permission. They didn't have money to buy things they needed or wanted. Their bodies belonged to their owners just as much as the bodies of the poorly treated slaves did. Many slave owners didn't think that slaves were smart enough to hope. We know, however, that many slaves never gave up their hope of being free.

Children of early slaves had very hard lives. They had few fun things to do. Their toys, if any, were homemade. There were no schools for them, no teachers, and no books. Even so, many slave children learned how to read.

From age six or seven, most slave children worked from sunrise until sunset. Children fed and cared for

farm animals. They ran errands, carried water, and cared for younger children. Many pulled weeds, picked bugs or worms off crops, and picked cotton.

Slave children **experienced** hardships that American children of today cannot imagine. Many were bought and sold as pets are today. But they were not given the care that pets ordinarily receive. Slave owners often bought whole families. Just as often, they bought only a father, mother, or child. Some family members lived on different plantations that were close to each other. Some lived in different cities or states.

Slaves on a cotton plantation

Sometimes after a family member was sold, the rest of the family never saw or heard from that person again.

Slaves were often beaten for oversleeping or for being too tired or sick to work. Some slaves were branded like cattle or scarred through whippings on their bare backs. Others were punished in even harsher ways. It is not surprising that so many slaves tried to escape to freedom. ✳

A newspaper ad offering a reward for the return of five runaway slaves

$200 Reward.

RANAWAY from the subscriber, on the night of Thursday, the 30th of Sepember,

FIVE NEGRO SLAVES,

To-wit : one Negro man, his wife, and three children.

The man is a black negro, full height, very erect, his face a little thin. He is about forty years of age, and calls himself *Washington Reed*, and is known by the name of Washington. He is probably well dressed, possibly takes with him an ivory headed cane, and is of good address. Several of his teeth are gone.

Mary, his wife, is about thirty years of age, a bright mulatto woman, and quite stout and strong.

The oldest of the children is a boy, of the name of FIELDING, twelve years of age, a dark mulatto, with heavy eyelids. He probably wore a new cloth cap.

MATILDA, the second child, is a girl, six years of age, rather a dark mulatto, but a bright and smart looking child.

MALCOLM, the youngest, is a boy, four years old, a lighter mulatto than the last, and about equally as bright. He probably also wore a cloth cap. If examined, he will be found to have a swelling at the navel.

Washington and Mary have lived at or near St. Louis, with the subscriber, for about 15 years.

It is supposed that they are making their way to Chicago, and that a white man accompanies them, that they will travel chiefly at night, and most probably in a covered wagon.

A reward of $150 will be paid for their apprehension, so that I can get them, if taken within one hundred miles of St. Louis, and $200 if taken beyond that, and secured so that I can get them, and other reasonable additional charges, if delivered to the subscriber, or to THOMAS ALLEN, Esq., at St. Louis. Mo. The

❋ Chapter 2 ❋
The Roads Runaways Traveled

By the late 1700s, most states in the northern part of the United States had become free states. They did not allow slavery. States in the South did allow slavery. **Fugitive** slave laws made it legal for slave-catchers to take black people who could not prove they were legally free. Because of these laws, many free blacks were kidnapped and sold into slavery.

Slaves hoped and dreamed and whispered about escaping. Their escape **routes** wound throughout the United States and Canada. They escaped from Louisiana, Georgia, Alabama, Mississippi, and South Carolina. The states that did not border free states were called the **Deep South.** A runaway often had to cross more than one state to get to freedom. Many tried, and some made it. Some escaped by boat from Florida to Cuba, the Bahaman Islands, Jamaica, and Haiti, where they believed they could be free.

Map labels: CANADA, WASHINGTON TERRITORY, OREGON, DAKOTA TERRITORY, MINN., WIS., MICH., N.Y., VT., ME., N.H., MASS., R.I., CONN., NEVADA TERR., UTAH TERRITORY, NEBRASKA TERRITORY, IOWA, PENN., N.J., COLORADO TERRITORY, ILL., IND., OHIO, DEL., MD., CALIFORNIA, KANSAS, MO., KENTUCKY, VIRGINIA, PACIFIC OCEAN, NEW MEXICO TERRITORY, INDIAN TERRITORY, ARK., TENN., N.C., S.C., MISS., GA., ALA., ATLANTIC OCEAN, TEXAS, LA., FLA., MEXICO, Gulf of Mexico

Slave states
Free states

0 200 400 miles
0 200 400 kilometers

N

   The Seminole American Indians sheltered and
protected hundreds of runaway slaves. Some of these
runaways married Seminoles and adopted their
customs. They fought with the Seminole chief Osceola
against General Andrew Jackson in the War of 1819.

   Other slaves climbed the Smoky Mountains of
North Carolina and mixed with Cherokee Indians.
Some slaves traveled across the wide-open plains of
Illinois, through Detroit, Michigan, to Canada.

   Canada was a safe place for runaways. Canadians
did not obey fugitive slave laws. They often attacked
slave-catchers or put them in jail. Runaways from the
South settled in parts of Canada and became Canadian

10

citizens. They started schools, churches, and all kinds of businesses. It was different in the United States. United States laws protected slave owners, not the runaways. The laws were especially harsh on free blacks who helped runaways.

Anyone who helped runaways could be punished. Even so, people of all colors helped runaway slaves. Southern whites who did not believe in slavery helped runaways before and after fugitive slave laws were passed. Members of many churches helped runaways. The Quakers, also known as the Society of Friends, were the first people to publicly declare that slavery was wrong. Many Quakers became **abolitionists.**

Abolitionists were not unlawful citizens, even though they sometimes disobeyed the slavery laws. Abolitionists were brave people who did not believe in slavery. They put their own lives in danger by helping runaways.

A Quaker named Isaac T. Hopper was a teenager in Philadelphia when he set up a system for hiding and helping runaway slaves. He probably didn't know that his system would one day be known as the Underground Railroad. Hopper became a famous abolitionist.

Many people believe that a Kentucky slave owner, not Hopper, came up with the name *Underground Railroad.* The slave owner rowed across the Ohio River to chase a runaway slave. The runaway, a man named Tice Davids, swam for his life. When he reached the banks of the Ohio, he disappeared. His owner couldn't find him. No one would admit that they had seen him.

The man later told friends that Davids disappeared as if he had found an "underground road." News of the events soon spread, and people began to use the name *Underground Railroad. Underground* was a good word to use because of the secrecy and mystery that escaping runaways needed in order to reach freedom. *Road* became *Railroad* to honor the new steam train that everybody was talking about in 1830.

The Underground Railroad was not a railroad. It was not a long tunnel under the ground. It was a system of directions for runaways, who traveled mostly on foot. The directions let runaways know how to get from one secret place to the next.

Besides *railroad,* other railway terms were also used. People who helped runaways by showing them the way to freedom were called **conductors.**

THE UNDERGROUND RAILROAD

CANADA

Scale:
0 — 150 — 300 miles
0 — 150 — 300 kilometers

MAINE

MINNESOTA

DAKOTA TERR.

WISCONSIN

MICHIGAN

NEW YORK

VT.

N.H.

MASS.

CONN.

R.I.

Mississippi River

Missouri River

IOWA

NEBRASKA TERR.

ILLINOIS

IND.

OHIO

PENN.

N.J.

MD.

DEL.

Ohio River

KANSAS

MISSOURI

KENTUCKY

VIRGINIA

Appalachian Mountains

Blue Ridge Mountains

INDIAN TERRITORY

ARKANSAS

TENNESSEE

Smoky Mountains

NORTH CAROLINA

SOUTH CAROLINA

Red River

Mississippi River

MISS.

ALABAMA

GEORGIA

ATLANTIC OCEAN

TEXAS

LOUISIANA

FLORIDA

Gulf of Mexico

N

Underground Railroad
Map shows boundaries of 1861.

13

A **station** was a place where fugitives could hide. Stations included barns and cellars and secret rooms in people's homes. Churches and businesses were also used as stations. At stations runaways were fed, clothed, and given a place to sleep. They were hidden until it was safe to go on to the next station.

People in charge of stations were called **station masters.** Fugitive slave laws gave slave-catchers the right to search people's homes and barns—even in free states. One station master hid three runaways under her mattress. She made up the bed as usual. When the slave-catchers came to search her home, they looked under the bed. They did not find the runaways.

This house in New York was a station on the Underground Railroad.

✳ Chapter 3 ✳
Freedom at Any Cost

Many slaves didn't use the Underground Railroad because their life was in danger. They ran without a plan. Many others did not know about the Underground Railroad or how to use it.

Even slaves that were fairly comfortable wanted to be in charge of their own life. They thought of ways to be free. Henry "Box" Brown chose a risky way to freedom. Henry's owner hired him out to work in a tobacco factory and demanded $275 of Henry's yearly wages. The man who owned Henry's wife, Nancy, took $50 of Henry's money every year. Henry and Nancy would not have been allowed to live together if Henry had refused to pay. Even so, Henry and Nancy raised two boys and saved $125 during their twelve years of marriage. Henry's hope was to save enough money to buy his family's freedom.

One day Henry came home from work and found that his family was gone! Nancy's owner had sold her and the two boys. Henry's friend, Samuel Smith, was a free man and a conductor on the Underground Railroad. He offered to help Henry escape. Henry then came up with a plan. He paid a man to build a wooden crate 3 feet long, 2½ feet wide, and 2½ feet deep. Henry was 5 feet, 8 inches tall.

Henry bored three tiny air holes in the top of the crate, where his head would be. Then he filled a leather pouch with water and stuffed a few biscuits in his pocket. He curled himself up in the box and said to Smith, "I can stand it for two or three days."

Smith nailed the box shut and addressed it to the office of an anti-slavery group in Philadelphia, Pennsylvania. This group included a well-known abolitionist named William Still. Samuel Smith wrote on the box "THIS SIDE UP WITH CARE."

Henry's box was taken by wagon to a boat and put aboard. Once he almost died from lack of air when the box was turned upside-down. Three days later, he was taken off the boat at Washington, D.C., and put on a train. His box arrived in Philadelphia one day

Henry "Box" Brown
arriving in Pennsylvania

late, but abolitionist William Still and his friends
rescued Henry. Henry was very thirsty and dirty,
but alive.

The fugitive slave law passed in 1850 stated that
slaves found in free states had to be returned to their
owners. Henry Brown left for Canada. He told his story
to William Still, who recorded it in his book, *The
Underground Railroad,* published in 1871. In this book
Still wrote about the narrow escapes of slaves in their
flight to freedom.

❄ Chapter 4 ❄
On the Run

Runaways needed to know how to survive if they hoped to escape from states that were far from free states. Sometimes their journey took months. They held secret meetings and learned codes and signals. A lighted candle in a station window meant it was safe to stop there. A dark window told runaways to hide or go to the next stop. Slaves and people who helped runaways also made quilts with codes sewn into patterns. These quilts were hung on clotheslines in certain ways.

Runaways had to remember that the sun rises in the east and sets in the west. They studied the stars and used the night sky as a guide. They learned about plants, berries, flowers, and roots that could be eaten or used for medicine. They also learned how to **predict** weather by reading cloud formations. They learned how to find caves and safe places to sleep. They had to remember that moss grows only on the north side of trees.

American Indians who lived in the mountains and on the plains taught runaways how to survive in the wilderness. They taught the runaways how to catch fish and trap small animals.

Jeb, a Kentucky slave, had to live in the woods for a long time. His story is an example of the hardships many runaways suffered. Jeb had run away and had been caught and returned to his owner. The owner punished Jeb very harshly. But one taste of freedom let Jeb know that he could not live the life of a slave any longer, so he ran away again.

Barking dogs woke Jeb one morning. He knew what their barking meant. Slave-catchers were on his trail!

A runaway trying to escape from slave-catchers

Jeb ran to the banks of a nearby stream. He waded into the water, taking a hollow reed with him. Then he stretched out and hid himself completely under the cold, muddy water. To breathe, he stuck one end of the reed in his mouth and made sure the other end stayed above the water.

Jeb stayed under the water while the dogs and slave-catchers searched the banks of the stream. After they left, he waded out and scrambled ashore. He ran for days, keeping the North Star over his left shoulder at night to guide him. He lived in caves and hid in barns. He was hungry most of the time. One day he ate poisonous berries by accident and almost died. His clothes grew ragged and filthy. A slave felt sorry for him and gave him a better pair of pants. A servant girl saw him and gave him table scraps meant for the chickens. A Quaker woman gave him a coat.

Jeb finally reached the Ohio River. He looked across and saw a small light **flickering** in the darkness. He knew that the light meant freedom! He slipped into the dark water and swam for what seemed like hours. He crawled up the banks of the Ohio River. He was very tired but full of hope.

Runaway slaves at a station on the Underground Railroad

Using the secret code he knew, Jeb rapped on the lighted window. A Quaker family let him in and gave him food, water, and clothes. One son made a bed of straw for Jeb in the secret bottom part of their wagon. Then he drove Jeb to another family's home, where Jeb hid in a barn. The next night Jeb was driven another 30 miles (48 kilometers). Not long after that, Jeb hid among sacks of grain and was **smuggled** aboard a ship bound for Canada. Finally he stepped off the ship in Canada. Jeb was a free man. ✳

Chapter 5

Heroes of the Underground Railroad

Dr. Alexander Ross from Ontario, Canada, was a **naturalist.** His job was studying nature, but he came to the United States to help slaves escape to freedom. He had learned about slavery in England and from runaways themselves. He traveled all over the South, studying birds, plants, and soil. His real purpose was finding friends of the Underground Railroad and finding the safest routes to Canada. He studied communities and held secret meetings.

At one meeting nine young men said they wanted to be free. Dr. Ross gave each one money, a pocket compass, a knife, a pistol, cold meat, and bread. Even more important, he told them about a route through Pennsylvania to Lake Erie and Canada. All nine reached Canada safely to become free men.

Dr. Ross devoted his life to helping slaves escape. He taught hundreds how to use the Underground Railroad.

This knowledge gave people the courage they needed to escape.

Writer and abolitionist Harriet Beecher Stowe wrote a book called *Uncle Tom's Cabin*. Published in 1852, Stowe's book made many people aware of the terrible way slaves lived. To many people who were against slavery, Stowe was a hero.

Dr. Alexander Ross

Other people said the book made the disagreements between the North and South worse. They claimed that the book started the Civil War. Many Southern people made a living by using slaves to do their work. Some Southerners hated Harriet Beecher Stowe because she used her writing to help slaves.

Harriet Beecher Stowe

Few slaves escaped from the Deep South because it was a long and very dangerous journey. But some were willing to take any chance for freedom. William and Ellen Craft were slaves in Georgia. William was a carpenter whose owner allowed him to keep all but $225 of his wages. Ellen sewed for her owner. They made a daring escape by **disguising** Ellen as a white man traveling with his servant.

As part of the Crafts' plan for escape, William bought gentleman's clothes for Ellen. Their thousand-mile journey began in December with three-day passes to visit relatives. Ellen pretended to be sick. Bandages hid her beardless face. Ellen looked white, but she had lived the simple life of a slave girl. Her right arm was in a sling to hide the fact that she could not write.

The Crafts traveled from Georgia to South Carolina and spent the night at Hotel Charleston. They paid for a first-class sleeping space for Ellen and traveled by boat and train to Philadelphia. William slept in the baggage car. During the trip, Ellen pretended to be hard of hearing to avoid talking to passengers and answering questions. She kept up this **pretense** for three days and nights.

In Philadelphia a **porter** offered to hide William and help him escape. William turned the man down, saying that his master needed him. The unbelieving porter told him to go to 31 North Fifth Street if he needed friends. That's exactly where William and his "master" went.

Ellen Craft

William Craft later wrote the incredible story of his and Ellen's escape to freedom. His book, *Running a Thousand Miles for Freedom,* was published in 1860 after he and Ellen moved to London.

Perhaps the most famous abolitionists were Frederick Douglass and Harriet Tubman. Both were born into slavery, and both escaped by the Underground Railroad.

Frederick Douglass operated an Underground Railroad station at his home in Rochester, New York, for many years after he ran away from his owner. He was called the Black Lion because of his fierce **determination** to free people from slavery.

Douglass was born as Frederick Bailey in 1818 on the shore of Tuckahoe Creek in eastern Maryland. His mother, Harriet Bailey, lived and worked on a farm too far away for her to visit often. Douglass's grandmother, Betsy, cared for him until he was old enough to work. When Douglass was about seven years old, she packed him up and walked him to Wye House, the plantation of his owner, Aaron Anthony. That was where Douglass's training was to begin. Anthony also owned Douglass's older sisters and brothers.

The head cook at Wye House took care of the children. Twice a day

A young Frederick Douglass

she gave them corn meal mush, which was served in a wooden **trough** set out in the yard. The children used seashells for spoons. Douglass slept in a potato sack next to the fireplace. He missed his grandmother, the comfort of her cabin, and her loving care. He saw his mother only once or twice after he moved to Wye House. She died shortly after. The cook at Anthony's house didn't like Douglass and sometimes whipped him or starved him for little reason.

Aaron Anthony's daughter, Lucretia, was married to Thomas Auld. Lucretia liked Douglass and treated him kindly. She secretly fed him and gave him an occasional treat. To protect Douglass from the cook, Lucretia and Thomas Auld sent him to Baltimore to live with Thomas's brother, Hugh Auld.

Hugh's wife, Sophia, knew nothing about slavery and treated Douglass like family. She taught him how to speak correctly and how to read. Five years went by. Although Douglass knew it was not **lawful,** he taught his black friends to read. He began to wonder about the slavery system in the United States. Soon he was reading every book and newspaper he could get his hands on.

Frederick Douglass in later years

Douglass was suddenly called back to Wye House when his owner, Aaron Anthony, died. Lucretia **inherited** Douglass as her part of her father's estate. Lucretia died not long afterward. Her husband, Thomas, inherited Douglass and hired him out. For five years Douglass learned what being a slave was all about. He grew to dislike Thomas Auld. When Douglass was nineteen, he and three friends spent time in jail for planning to run away. Thomas Auld sent him back to Baltimore to live with Sophia and Hugh Auld.

Douglass's Baltimore family was not the same. He was a grown man now. Miss Sophia hardly said anything to him. Her son, who had been like a brother, was neither friendly nor unfriendly. Hugh Auld found Douglass a job with a shipbuilder named William Gardiner. Of course, Auld kept Douglass's wages.

In the 1830s some white workers were not happy that a black person had a job when so many whites needed jobs. After a fight, Douglass was hurt badly. Auld would not let him go back to that job. He put Douglass to work in another shipyard. Auld kept all of Douglass's wages, which were $7 per week. After a time, this did not seem fair to either of them, so Auld let Douglass go out on his own. Douglass found a place to live and bought his own food and clothes. Auld took only $3 a week.

Douglass met and fell in love with free-born Anna Murray. Together they planned his escape. Douglass bought fake papers, borrowed clothes from a sailor friend, and took a train from Baltimore to New York City. Anna soon followed him, and they were married. He found a job in a shipyard. He studied hard and became an active abolitionist.

On December 5, 1846, two of Douglass's friends bought his freedom from Thomas Auld for $100. In the fall of 1847, Douglass began an anti-slavery newspaper, which he called *The North Star*. Later he wrote four books. He also became a very popular speaker for human rights.

Frederick Douglass in his
home in Washington, D.C.

Douglass became a friend and advisor to President Abraham Lincoln and held top political jobs under Presidents James A. Garfield, Benjamin Harrison, and Rutherford B. Hayes.

Douglass and Anna had four children, whom he loved dearly. Anna died on August 4, 1882, at age 69. Douglass was 64. In 1884 he married Helen Pitts, an abolitionist and business associate. Frederick Douglass died February 20, 1895, at the age of 87.

Harriet Tubman was perhaps the most beloved conductor of the Underground Railroad. She helped many people escape to freedom. She carried a pistol in her pocket and threatened to use it if runaways got cold

feet and wanted to turn back. Turning back might ruin the group's chance for escape. Tubman never lost a passenger.

Tubman's birth name was Araminta Ross. She was born about 60 miles south of Baltimore, Maryland, in 1820 or 1821. When she was six years old, she was put to work taking care of a younger child. When Tubman was a teenager, she stepped in front of an object that an overseer was throwing at another slave. Tubman's face and head were injured. As a result, she suffered severe headaches and blackouts for the rest of her life.

Tubman's mother, Harriet Ross, took loving care of her for six months. Tubman renamed herself Harriet to honor her mother. In 1844 she fell in love with a free black man named John Tubman and married him.

Harriet Tubman

When Tubman was a little girl, she saw two of her older sisters taken away by a slave trader. The memory of their frightened faces never faded. Tubman's young master died in 1849. When she found out she was about to be sold, she decided to run away. She knew that few people in Dorchester County could afford to buy slaves. She was afraid of being sold to someone in the Deep South, where she would have to pick cotton in the blazing sun. Neither her husband nor her brothers would go with her. Tubman had to leave the family she loved so much.

Tubman could not read or write, but she had a good mind. She had learned all she could about the Underground Railroad and people who had helped other slaves escape. She traveled the Underground Railroad by herself.

Tubman made it to Philadelphia. Two years later she went back to Maryland for her husband and found that he had married another woman. Marriage and divorce laws did not apply to slaves. John refused to leave his second wife.

Tubman risked her life at least nineteen times to go back to her old neighborhood. She led members of her

family and many more to freedom. She conducted some people all the way to Canada and helped them get settled. During the Civil War, she worked as a nurse and spy for the **Union** Army. Tubman died in 1913 and was buried in Auburn, New York. Loved by many, she was a woman who journeyed with great courage. ✳

Tubman with slaves she helped to escape

Afterword

President Abraham Lincoln's Emancipation Proclamation of June, 1863, was meant to free the slaves in all states at war with the Union, but it did not. The slaves were not freed until the Civil War ended on April 9, 1865. The Underground Railroad stopped. Unequal treatment of black people did not.

Discrimination against black people because of their color continued for another hundred years. In 1964, under pressure from President Lyndon B. Johnson and the movement led by Dr. Martin Luther King, Jr., Congress finally passed the Civil Rights Bill. This law **banned** discrimination in public places, schools, housing, and jobs.

The heroes of the Underground Railroad believed in freedom for all people and were willing to risk their own freedom and life to help others.

Reading about the Underground Railroad helps us understand more about the United States. It also helps us when we think about the future. By learning from what happened in the past, we can make sure that we do not repeat its mistakes.

Glossary

abolitionists (a buh LISH uh nists) people who wanted to end slavery in the United States in the years before the Civil War

banned (band) forbid by law; made illegal

bondage (BAHN dij) slavery

conductors (kuhn DUHK tuhrz) people who helped runaway slaves by showing them the way to freedom

customs (KUHS tuhmz) the usual ways of acting that go on over long periods of time

Deep South (deep sowth) the states of Louisiana, Mississippi, Alabama, Georgia, North Carolina, and South Carolina

determination (dih tuhr muh NAY shuhn) great firmness in carrying something out; a strong purpose

discrimination (dis KRIM uh NAY shun) the act or policy of treating people unfairly because of their color, race, religion, nationality, sex, or age

disguising (dis GYZ ing) changing the way one looks

experienced (ik SPIHR ee uhnst) went though; had happen to

flickering (FLIK uhr ing) shining or glowing with an uneven light

flight (flyt) the act of running away to be free; escape

fugitive (FYOO jih tiv) a person who is running away or has run away, especially someone trying to escape from the law

indentured (in DEN chuhrd) bound by a contract in which one person agrees to serve another for a certain period of time

inherited (in HEHR it id) received money, property, or personal belongings from someone who has died

intelligent (in TEL uh juhnt) able to use the mind well; smart

lawful (LAW ful) allowed by the law; legal

naturalist (NACH ruhl ist) a person who studies nature, especially one who studies plants and animals living in nature

plantations (plan TAY shunz) large farms where one crop is grown, and the work is done by workers who live there

porter (PAWR tuhr) a person hired to carry luggage or packages; a person who helps passengers on a train

predict (pri DIKT) to tell about something that will happen

pretense (PREE tens) a false appearance or action

profitable (PRAHF it uh buhl) money-making

routes (rowts or roots) ways to get from place to place; roads or paths

slavery (SLAYV ree) the practice of owning another person who can be sold like a piece of property

smuggled (SMUHG uhld) carried or taken secretly

station (STAY shun) a stopping place along the Underground Railroad

station masters (STAY shun MAS tuhrz) people in charge of stopping places on the Underground Railroad

tribe (tryb) a group of people who live in the same area and share the same language and customs

trough (trawf) a long, narrow container used for feeding or watering farm animals

Union (YOO yuhn) the northern and border states in the Civil War

wages (WAY jez) payment for work done

Index

Suggested Reading

Ball, Charles. *American Slavery.* Steck-Vaughn Publishing, 1995

Bial, Raymond. *The Underground Railroad.* Houghton Mifflin, 1995

Blockson, Charles L. *The Underground Railroad.* Prentice Hall, 1987

Buckmaster, Henrietta. *Flight to Freedom.* Dell, 1958

Davidson, Basil. *The African Slave Trade 1450–1850.* Little Brown, 1961

Davis and Gates. *The Slave's Narrative.* Oxford University Press, 1985

Dumond, Dwight Lowell. *Antislavery.* University of Michigan Press, 1961

King, Wilma. *Toward the Promised Land.* Chelsea House, 1995

McFeely, William S. *Frederick Douglass.* W.W. Norton, 1991

McKissack, Patricia and Frederick. *Frederick Douglass.* Children's Press, 1944

Muelder, Hermann Richard. *Fighters for Freedom.*
    Columbia University Press, 1959

National Geographic Magazine. July, 1984

Official National Park Service Handbook No.156,
    Underground Railroad. U.S. Department of
    the Interior, 1998

Peferdehirt, Julia. *Freedom Train North.* Living
    History Press, 1998

Smucker, Barbara. *Runaway to Freedom.* Harper
    and Row, 1977

Still, William. *The Underground Railroad.* Johnson
    Publishing, 1970

Stowe, Harriet B. *Uncle Tom's Cabin.* Henry
    Altemus, 1895

Turner, Glennette Tilley. *The Underground
    Railroad in Illinois.* Newman Educational
    Publishers, 2002

Winter, Jeanette. *Follow The Drinking Gourd.*
    Alfred A. Knopf, 1988

Wright, Courtni C. *Journey to Freedom.* Holiday
    House, 1994